THE WAR BEGAN AT SUPPER

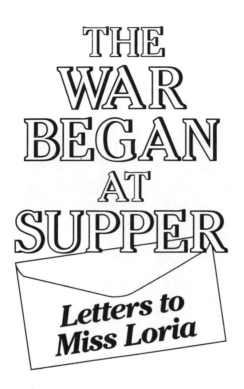

Letters to Miss Loria

THE WAR BEGAN AT SUPPER

Letters to Miss Loria

Patricia Reilly Giff

illustrated by Betsy Lewin

DELACORTE PRESS

Published by
Delacorte Press
Bantam Doubleday Dell Publishing Group, Inc.
666 Fifth Avenue
New York, New York 10103

A special thank-you to the second-grade children of the
Coleytown School...and to their teachers:
Jane Fraser
Anne Nesbitt
Donna Skolnick

ISBN: 0-385-30530-3

Manufactured in the United States of America

June 1991

10 9 8 7 6 5 4 3 2 1

BVG

Love to my children:
Jim and Laura, Bill and Cathie, and Alice
And to their children:
Jimmy and Chris, and our June baby

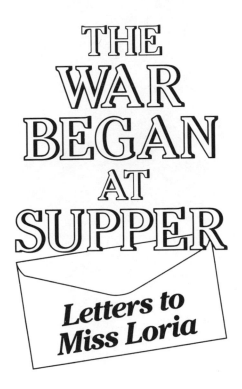

THE WAR BEGAN AT SUPPER

Letters to Miss Loria

Sara

◆   Sara   ◆

Wednesday, January 2

Dear Miss Loria,

This is the letter I promised to send you.

I miss you.

You were the best student teacher I had in my whole life.

The class said to say hello.

Jessica said she's going to write too.

So did Michael M. and Karl.

(Don't count on Karl. All he thinks about is making jokes and fooling around with his dog, Bigfoot.)

HAPPY NEW YEAR.

Love,
Sara

P.S. Did you know we might have a war?
Mrs. Clark said.

1

Michael M.

◆   ◆

Friday, January 4

Dear Miss Loria,

Remember me? I'm Michael M. (Not Michael S. next to the window.)

I have news.

It's about my father.

He may be going to a place called the Persian Gulf.

He is in the reserves. That means he goes away to practice about war on weekends.

This time it may not be a practice.

He has a uniform. You know, the kind with brown and tan blobs all over it?

My mother was crying in the closet when she heard about the war.

I told her don't worry.

Write back soon.

Your friend,
Michael M.

Jessica

Dear Miss Loria,

Sara showed your letter to everyone in the class.

I loved the pink writing paper with the kittens on top.

It was the paper I gave you for Christmas. Remember?

Sara said she didn't think so.

I said it was so. It was definitely so.

Mrs. Clark put the letter on the bulletin board.

She said Sara should stop shaking her head a hundred times.

She said I should stop saying yes a hundred times.

She said Sara and I better not sit together anymore.

Sara was crying. She's such a baby.

Did you hear about the war?

Mrs. Clark thinks it might happen any minute.

It's far away, so don't worry.

XXXXX,

Jessica

(Your best friend in Mrs. Clark's class.)

3

Alice

Dear Miss Loria,

How are you? Everyone is writing to you. I thought I would too. (This is Alice. The one who loves reading and peanut butter.)

Everyone is talking about a war. It's against someone named Saddam Hussein. He has a mustache and a uniform, and I think he's supposed to be crazy.

My mother and father watch the news every second. My father even brought the little TV down to his workroom last night.

Something else. My mother and father are fighting about the war, yelling. My mother said we shouldn't go to war, we should mind our own business, and not send soldiers to fight over oil in a place nobody even cares about.

"I care," said my father. "We can't stand by and let someone gobble up the world."

Eric, my brother, said he wished they'd stop arguing.

Then my mother and father got mad at Eric.

"That's the beauty of being American," my mother said. "You can say exactly what you please."

Eric said he can't say exactly what he pleases.

My mother and father laughed.

Eric says there isn't going to be a war anyway. Everyone is talking it over. The President. The people at the United Nations.

I hope Eric is right. I don't even know what this whole thing is all about.

Yours truly,
Alice

Jessica

Friday, January 11

Dear Miss Loria,

I thought you might want to see this right away. Mrs. Clark told us to write about current events.

Sara wrote about the free pretzel sticks they're giving out at the new delicatessen. (Not too good.) Karl wrote about his dog. (Terrible, but funny anyway.)

Mrs. Clark said mine was excellent. See the star and VERY GOOD on top? I think it was the best in the class.

Love,
Jessica

7

★ Very Good

Jessica Redman   Writing

The War

We may be going to have a war in Iraq. It is
because Saddam Hussein went into a country that
does not belong to him. The country is called
Kuwait. It has a lot of oil. We feel sorry for the
people. We need the oil. Saddam Hussein is mean
to them. He will keep the oil all to himself.
President Bush told him to get out of there by
January 15. If he doesn't go, we will send out
soldiers.

Michael M.

♦   ♦

Friday, January 11

Dear Miss Loria,

My father let me try on his gas mask.

It is cool.

It's heavy though, and I felt as if I couldn't breathe.

I wanted to bring it to school, but my father said no way.

From,
Michael

Sara

Dear Miss Loria,

Everyone is hoping there won't be a war.

A bunch of high school kids stood in front of Fairside Store with signs.

One sign said PEACE NOT WAR.

Another sign said HONK FOR PEACE.

A lot of cars honked when they went by.

You could hear them all the way down Post Road.

Jackie Mines has a horn on his bike. He honked too.

Love,
Sara

P.S. Remember that pen I gave you for Christmas? Do you get to use it when you write letters?

10

◆ A Note from Jessica ◆

Tuesday, January 15

Dear Miss Loria,

I got these cards for my birthday on Sunday. (You don't have to send a present.) Thanks for writing back. Thanks for saying it was my writing paper from Christmas. Sara said she gave you a pen. She said it was blue, exactly the same color as your coat with the silver buttons. (I think you like pink a little bit better than blue. Right?) My father was in another war. He said it was terrible.

Love,
Jessica

Wednesday, January 16

Dear Miss Loria,

Michael M.'s father went to Saudi Arabia yesterday.

Saudi Arabia is a neighbor to Iraq. We saw it on a map.
Mrs. Clark says it's a desert place with camels. People
wrap cloths around their heads to stay cool.

Michael M. stayed home from school. He went to the
airport to wave good-bye.

He said his grandmother was crying all over the place.
He said she kept saying we should have peace.

Michael says that's because she remembers another
war. She knew someone who won a medal called a Purple
Heart because he hurt his leg. She says he still walks with
a cane.

Everyone else was crying too.

Everyone except Michael.

He wishes he could be a soldier too.

Besides, he says his father is coming right home
anyway. He'd never miss Michael's birthday in February.

And do you know what Karl said?

He told us his aunt is going to go to the war.

That Karl. He doesn't know anything.

Women don't go to war, do they?

If my mother went to war, it would be terrible. It would be the worst thing that ever happened to me.

Love,
Sara

◆ A Note from Jessica ◆

Dear Miss Loria,

I told Sara your favorite color is pink. She keeps shaking her head.

Please put an X in the blank.

Favorite color:

Pink _____

Any other color _____

XXXOOO
Jessica

Thursday, January 17

Dear Miss Loria,

A war got started while we were having supper last night. I saw a little of it on television. The newsman held a microphone out a hotel window so we could hear the bombs.

Then my mother said let's go to church.

My mother and father, my brother and I went.

There were other people too.

The church looked beautiful. It was all dark with candles.

Father Kinsella prayed that the war would be over soon. He prayed that our soldiers would be all right. Then we sang a hymn. We sang "God Bless America."

I think my father had tears in his eyes. Isn't that funny? I never saw my father cry before. He and my mother were holding hands.

This morning Mr. Brancato next door put a flag up on his front porch.

Yours truly,
Alice

Karl

◆   ◆

Thursday, January 17

Dear Miss Loria,
There is a war on now. It looks a little like Nintendo
on TV.

From,
Karl

Sara

◆   ◆

Thursday, January 17

Dear Miss Loria,
    Something else terrible happened today. Something
besides the war.
    We have a new delicatessen. (I wrote about it for
current events.)
    Today I went for my free pretzel stick.
    The window had a big crack in it.
    Mrs. Hammadi told me someone had thrown a stone.

16

She said it was because she came from Iraq. But she says she came a long time ago.

She says she is American.

Someone phoned her. He didn't say what his name was. He said she should go back to Iraq.

I feel sad for Mrs. Hammadi. I think it isn't fair.

Sara

Michael M.

♦   ♦

Thursday, January 17

Dear Miss Loria,

It's me Michael again. Well, we are at war with Iraq.

Right now airplanes are bombing everything.

If the soldiers on the ground move in, my father will move in too.

We saw all about the planes and bombs on TV.

Flashes of light were popping all over the sky.

My mother sat on the couch and watched.

She used a whole box of tissues.

I don't know why she's crying. My father is going to wipe out the whole Iraqi army.

He'll be home in plenty of time for my birthday. (31 more days. I counted on the kitchen calendar.)

I think we will have a party. Maybe he will let me keep his gas mask.

Your friend,
Michael

◆   Sara   ◆

Friday, January 18

Dear Miss Loria,

I'm really really afraid of the war. Last night I saw some of the war on television. There were streets and buildings just like here.

One hotel even looked just like the place where we stayed last summer. I tried to picture our beach with bombs in it.

I tried to picture my house and my bedroom.

18

I could hear noise on television. Someone said it was missiles. They sounded like static on the radio. Not like bombs.

When I went to bed I kept listening.

I was glad my mother and father were in the living room.

Suppose a missile came?

Suppose it landed on my street?

If my mother and father were hurt, what would I do?

Love,
Sara

P.S. I'm glad you're using my pen. Did you tell Jessica?

Saturday, January 19

Dear Miss Loria,

Thank you for your letter. I love that pink paper with the kittens. I cut out the kitten with the bow.

Guess where it's going? All the way to the war.

Mrs. Clark told us we could write to a soldier. We don't even have to know his name. The post office will give us the address.

It's strange to write to someone you never even saw before.

I've been trying to think of something to say.

I think he will like the kitten anyway.

Yours truly,
Alice

◆ A Note from Jessica ◆

Dear Miss Loria,

We are still working on our word lists, just like when you were here. I have the most words. I think Sara is trying to get ahead of me now. You should see Michael's list. It's all about war. I'm going to tell him to send some words to you. Karl has two words. They're both spelled wrong. My new word is FORTUNE. It's not about war. It's about having something great, like a lot of money.

Love,
Jessica

Tuesday, January 22

Dear Miss Loria,

Did you hear about the terrorists? They bomb everything.

I think they might bomb my school bus.

I'm going to walk.

Don't worry. I can make it.

From,

Karl

Michael M.

Thursday, January 24

Dear Miss Loria,

Here is my word list.

Jessica said you were dying to see it.

SORTIE—means 1 of our planes goes to a target like a germ factory and bombs it.

GAS MASK—a thing you put on your face in case they shoot germs in a missile. Then you can breathe good fresh air.

SCUD MISSILES—are missiles that Iraqis shoot. They can travel about 400 miles, then BOOM.

PATRIOT MISSILES—belong to our guys. They shoot down Scuds and enemy planes.

(I didn't send my whole list. Before the war it was boring.)

Your friend,
Michael

Thursday, January 24

Dear Miss Loria,

I watched TV last night. I saw a house all wrecked from bombs. I saw children crying and a mother too. The mother's hands were up in the air. I almost started to cry too.

My mother told me to turn off the TV.

She went into her bedroom. She brought out a paper bag from the Fairside Store.

It had a lot of yellow ribbon in it.

We went outside in the dark. It wasn't very dark though. The stars were out and the moon. You could see all the snow piled up, and our breath in the air.

We picked a tree and wrapped the ribbon around it. Then we tied a bow.

My mother told me it meant we were thinking about the soldiers.

She said to look at the ribbon.

She said to think about when everyone would come

home and the missiles would stop and the war would
be over.

A little snip of ribbon was left over. I pinned it on my
jacket.

Love,
Sara

Karl

Dear Miss Loria,

I walked to school. It took a long time. I was late.

But the worst part was my dog, Bigfoot, kept
following me.

Bigfoot is the greatest dog in the world.

I kept telling him to go home.

I don't want him to get lost.

He wouldn't go home though. He played in the school
yard all day.

I saw the custodian go outside to chase him away, but he came right back.

I was worried about him. I kept sharpening my pencil so I could look out the window.

I was glad to go home.

Don't tell anyone about this, please.

From,
Karl

♦ Alice ♦

Dear Miss Loria,

A lot has happened since I wrote to you. Don't worry that I'm writing 2X and you wrote only 1X. I know you are busy in your new school.

Guess what?

I got a letter from the soldier.

I read it in class.

The soldier's name is Helen Denning.

She's a woman soldier.

As soon as Sara heard that, she started to cry.

Mrs. Clark kept saying what's the matter?

Sara wouldn't tell us though.

Mrs. Clark let me take her outside and we put water on a paper towel for Sara's face.

"Why don't you tell me why you're crying?" I asked Sara.

She kept shaking her head.

Then Karl came along. He was really late.

He's late every day.

I don't know what's the matter with him. He used to make a lot of jokes. Now he hardly talks.

I don't know what's the matter with Sara either.

Everyone is crazy lately.

Love,
Alice

♦ A Quick Note from Jessica ♦

Dear Miss Loria,
I HAVE FORTY-SEVEN WORDS ON MY LIST. DID YOU
FORGET TO FILL IN THE BLANKS ABOUT THE PINK
AND BLUE?

J.

♦ Michael M. ♦

Tuesday, January 29

Dear Miss Loria,
   You won't believe this.
   We saw my father on TV last night.
   A TV man was in Saudi Arabia. He had a microphone
and he was talking to all the soldiers.
   You could see a lot of sand and trucks and things.
   All the soldiers were smiling and waving.

And then there was my father, right in the middle of the picture.

He was on for only a half a second.

He looked as if the sun were in his eyes. He had a tan.

You know what? My mother was crying even harder. Her face is all red and her eyes are squinty from it. Even her voice sounds as if she has a cold.

My father is big and strong. He's going to win the war. I thought he'd be home by now though.

Do you think he's not going to be home by next week?

Suppose he misses my grandmother's birthday?

Suppose he misses mine?

Your friend,
Michael

A Note from Jessica

Thursday, January 31

Dear Miss Loria,

I guess you remember Sara and I aren't best friends anymore.

Sara doesn't even look at me.

She always has her nose in a book.

You know that long hair she has. It falls right over her face when she's reading.

She didn't even turn around when I threw her a let's make up note.

Too bad for Sara.

I threw the note in the garbage.

I heard you wrote to Alice and Michael.

You're writing a lot of letters LATELY. (Word list.)

If you need more paper, let me know. My mother got a whole pile on sale.

I haven't heard from you in a long time.

Your *best* friend,
Jessica

32

Alice

◆　　　　　　　　　　　　　　　　　　　　　　　　◆

Friday, February 1

Dear Miss Loria,

Here is the letter from Private Denning. She signed her name Helen, so that's what I'm calling her.

Mrs. Clark made a copy of the letter for everyone.

I think more kids are going to write to soldiers.

Love,
Alice

◆ Private Helen Denning ◆

ARMY
Operation Desert Shield
APO, N.Y. 09848-006

Dear Alice,

I was so happy to receive your letter. I really enjoyed seeing your picture of the cat with the bow.

33

We are all working hard here. The weather is miserable, hot and sticky. We practice every day so we will be just perfect when we need to be.

Don't worry, Alice. We are going to win this war. We're not going to let anybody down. We all want to do it, and do it fast, so we can come back home.

One reason I'm anxious to get home fast is the food. The army dinners taste a little like the food I feed my dog. They look like the food I feed my fish. (Joke.)

Say hello to your class.

Your new friend,
Helen Denning

◆ Sara ◆

Friday, February 1

Dear Miss Loria,

This afternoon Alice and Michael got into a fight.

We were on the way home and Alice said the war is going to last a long time... maybe all spring, maybe all

summer, maybe even longer. Her mother said. So did her father.

Michael said that was a big lie, that the war was almost over already.

He said he was going to tell his mother to bake a chocolate cake for his birthday. It's his father's favorite kind. He and his father are going to eat the whole thing together.

Alice didn't say anything. She shook her head a little. She kept rubbing her hands together because she was cold.

And do you know what Michael did?

He threw his reader in the middle of Mrs. Brancato's sticker bush.

I think Michael is getting very fresh.

Love,
Sara

Karl

Dear Miss Loria,

Bigfoot keeps following me to school.

I tell him to go home.

I even threw a stick. Not to hit him, of course. To make him think.

I really don't want him to go home though.

If a missile comes, we'll dive into the bushes. We'll hide there and be safe.

I'm not telling anyone else about this.

My aunt Ellen is a nurse. She may be going to the war. What would she think if she knew I was afraid?

Another thing. I'm worried about Bigfoot crossing Post Road.

There are lots of cars.

Bigfoot doesn't know about lights.

Sometimes he runs out. He likes to chase cars. He barks and jumps up trying to catch them.

I tell him you can get hurt that way.

From,
Karl

♦ A Note from Jessica ♦

Tuesday, February 5

Dear Miss Loria,

Thank you for your letter.

It's INTERESTING (word list) you like pink and blue
both the same.

I thought about showing your letter to Sara.

Then I heard something. Alice told me Sara's mother is
going to give her a Valentine's Day party.

I don't think Sara is going to invite me.

Don't worry, I don't mind. Maybe I'm going to go
somewhere else that night, like out with my mother
or something.

Love,
Jessica

P.S. I looked out the school-bus window this morning and
saw a million flags on houses and in the store windows.
Mrs. Hammadi from the deli was outside her house. She
was painting her mailbox red, white, and blue. Then the

bus passed Karl. I turned around and saw that the last
seat was empty. It's been empty every day lately. No
wonder Karl is so late to school.

♦   Sara   ♦

Tuesday, February 5

Dear Miss Loria,

    On Sunday, my mother and father went to a wedding.
They didn't invite kids.

    Instead Karen from next door came over.

    We turned on the television.

    A man was talking all about the war.

    I didn't understand one thing he was saying. He kept
talking about different kinds of planes and swordys.

    Then Karen heard a noise like SSSSSSSS BAM.

    "It's a bomb," Karen yelled.

    We raced downstairs to the basement.

    We couldn't hear one more thing, because my mother

39

had put sheets in the washing machine before she left.

We waited a long time. Then Karen said maybe we should go to the top of the stairs and just peek our heads out.

She said not to breathe in case it was a germ missile.

We tiptoed upstairs and Karen opened the door a crack.

For a moment I kept my eyes closed. I didn't know what it would look like up there.

When I opened my eyes, I could see the kitchen sink and the windowsill with my mother's African violet.

I could hear the man on the television, still talking about swordys.

"Come on," Karen said.

We took a step into the kitchen, then looked out the window.

A big clump of snow must have fallen off the roof onto the sidewalk. It wasn't a missile at all.

Love,
Sara

Michael M.

Tuesday, February 5

Dear Miss Loria,

My grandmother called my mother and said to turn on the television right away. She said some soldiers had been captured by the Iraqi army.

My mother raced down the stairs. She went so fast she tripped on her bathrobe and slid down on the bottom step.

I went around her.

"Turn on the television, Michael," she said. "Turn it on loud so I can hear it."

"Did you break your ankle or something?" I asked her.

She shook her head. "No," she said. "I just have to catch my breath."

I went into the living room.

For a minute I didn't want to turn on the television. Suppose my father had been captured?

What would they do to him?

Then I turned on the television as loud as I could. It was a cartoon. It blasted in my ears.

"No, Michael, not that," my mother yelled.

"I know, I know," I said. I fiddled with the knob until I got the news.

By the time the man told about the pilots, my mother had come into the living room. She was leaning on the door.

"Pilots," she said after a minute. "Not soldiers. Not Daddy."

"I knew it," I said. "I knew it wasn't Daddy."

My mother sat down on the couch. "It could have been." She rocked back and forth a little. "Poor families," she said. "Poor men."

I went into the kitchen and took out two bowls of cereal, one for me and one for my mom.

I poured in milk and took them into the living room.

"Oh, Michael," my mother said.

We sat there, and watched television, and ate our cereal.

I asked my mother whether the pilots had any children.

My mother shook her head. "I don't know."

I didn't say anything else. I didn't want her to start crying.

Your friend,
Michael

P.S. After lunch we got a letter from my father. The postman even banged on the door so we'd know right away. My father asked my mother to send him some more of the shaving stuff he likes. I guess he won't make it home for my birthday.

◆ # Karl ◆

Dear Miss Loria,

Thank you for your letter.

Don't worry about me walking to school.

I have a new way.

I cut through some backyards. (I can't do it all the way. Bigfoot can't climb over the fences.)

One thing wrong though.

It's Post Road.

Today, Bigfoot raced out in front of a red car.

The car brakes screeched.

I couldn't look for a minute.

Then I saw Bigfoot on the other side of the street. He was okay.

Mrs. Hammadi was outside her deli. She saw the whole thing.

She gave Bigfoot and me a pretzel.

She said maybe Bigfoot should stay home.

I didn't tell her about the terrorists. I didn't want to get her worried too.

How long do you think the war is going to go on?

From,
Karl

Dear Miss Loria,

The whole class was happy to get your letter.

I was surprised you thought we could do some things about the war.

I wish you had told me what to do.

It's hard to think of anything... but as soon as I do, I'll write back.

Someone came into our classroom the other day. Her name was Mrs. Baker.

She's the school psychologist. She wears culottes and lots of necklaces, and she jiggles the necklaces with her fingers when she talks.

She said she wanted to ask us how we felt about the war.

Everyone looked at Michael.

He's the most important because his father is in Saudi Arabia.

But Michael had to get a drink of water. He didn't come back until Mrs. Baker had gone.

Outside of Michael, everyone is afraid of the war.

I didn't know that.

I thought I was the only one.

Yours truly,
Alice

Sara

Dear Miss Loria,

Did you hear Mrs. Baker came to see us?

We talked for a long time about the war.

There wasn't even time for math.

When Mrs. Clark looked at the clock, she told us to hurry.

We grabbed our lunch and raced for the cafeteria.

We just made it in the door before the milk line ended.

We talked about Mrs. Baker all through lunch.

Did you know that Mrs. Baker was in a real war when she was a little girl?

She said there were bombs every night.

"After a while," she said, "we got used to it. We went to school, we played outside."

Mrs. Baker says that sometimes it's worse just imagining about things.

Maybe that's right.

I'm always afraid to go down to the basement alone.

I keep thinking someone's hiding behind the stairs...someone who's going to get me.

Then when I have to go down there, and I turn on the light, it's just the same old basement, and the same old stairs with my father's tools stacked up in the corner.

Love,
Sara

◆ A Note from Jessica ◆

Dear Miss Loria,

Guess what Mrs. Baker said?

First she asked us what a natural resource was.

I said it was trees and rivers and stuff like that, and Alice said it was things belonging to a country to make them rich.

"What's our most important resource?" Mrs. Baker asked next.

Everyone guessed a million things like gold and iron and stuff.

Mrs. Baker kept shaking her head no. "Wrong," she said. "It's you."

Us.

Isn't that a surprise?

We looked at Mrs. Clark. She was nodding her head.

"Don't worry," said Mrs. Baker. "We're going to protect our most important resources."

Karl was walking around waving his arms. He kept saying he was a tree. Sometimes Karl is funny.

Love,
Jessica

Karl

Tuesday, February 12

Dear Miss Loria,

Today I didn't have lunch.

Bigfoot was waiting for me across the street.

He doesn't come into the school yard anymore.

The custodian threw a paper at him.

First Bigfoot thought it was a game.

Then when he heard the man yell, he went over to Mrs. Weber's house.

Mrs. Weber goes to work like my mother.

She doesn't know Bigfoot is sitting on her step.

I sneaked out of school.

I gave my lunch to Bigfoot.

Then I thought what if a bomb came to Mrs. Weber's
house.

Bigfoot would be in big trouble.

He's my greatest natural resource.

From,

Karl

P.S. Don't worry about my lunch. It was the kind
of sandwich I hate— cream cheese.

♦ A Note from Jessica ♦

Wednesday, February 13

Dear Miss Loria,

Sara has NOT invited me to her Valentine party. I keep looking for a card in my desk, but it never comes.

Jessica

P.S. I was going to use INVITE for a word-list word. It makes me feel bad though.

Alice

Wednesday, February 13

Dear Miss Loria,

Sara's mother wants to give Sara a Valentine party. But Sara told me she's too afraid to think about a party. She thinks we might even be bombed by Valentine's Day.

I thought of one thing to do about the war, and I'm doing it already. Writing to Private Helen Denning. My mom and I sent her a book and some cookies.

I'm writing more letters too.

Mrs. Clark said it's good to tell people how we feel about things. We can even write to the President and tell him.

Karl says he's going to write and say he feels we should be off from school more.

But I'm going to write and tell him I'm worried about the war.

Jessica is going to write too. She wants him to know she has the biggest word list in the class. She also wants his autograph.

Love,
Alice

♦ A Note from Jessica ♦

Wednesday, again

Dear Miss Loria,

Something terrible happened to me. It is like the war.
It is worse than the war.

We had a substitute teacher.

I was trying to help her out. I told her where to hang
up her coat. I told her about the writing paper I gave you.
I told her about my word list, and the letter I wrote to the
President last week.

All of a sudden the substitute teacher told me to take
my seat. "Give someone else a chance," she said.

And someone said that's right, Jessica thinks she's Miss
Big in Mrs. Clark's class.

I sat down.

I didn't look at anybody.

Nobody looked at me.

Maybe people think I'm a pest like Saddam Hussein.

Love,
Jessica

Michael M.

Dear Miss Loria,

Last night I had a bad dream. It was the second time this week. It was about wearing a gas mask, and I couldn't breathe, and there was sand blowing all over the place.

When I woke up, I thought my father had been captured by Saddam Hussein. It was so dark in my room, I could hardly see.

Then my mother came in.

I told her I don't want my father to be in the war anymore. I just want him to come home.

My mother sat on the bed for a long time. She said she wants him to come home too.

We tried to figure out what time it was in Saudi Arabia. We thought my father must be just getting up. My mother said she knew he'd be thinking of us at the same minute.

I said I wondered if he remembered my birthday.

"Michael," she said, "you're the most important thing

in your father's life. Of course he remembers your
birthday."

I asked if we could have another cake when he comes
home. My mother said we'll have cake every day for
a week.

Your friend,
Michael

◆ # Sara ◆

Thursday, February 14

Dear Miss Loria,

Today Mrs. Clark talked about how far away Iraq is.
It's far. It really is.

Mrs. Clark has been saying that every day, but this time
she said it would take longer to get to than the North
Pole.

And that's really far.

Mrs. Clark said something else. She said to stop
worrying about the war so much.

She said our mothers and fathers will take care of us.

So will she.

And so will Private Denning.

I think I'm going to have a Valentine party.

My mother said I could invite everyone in the whole
class.

Love,
Sara

Jessica

Thursday, February 14

Dear Miss Loria,

I'm starting over.

I don't want to be like Saddam Hussein.

Even if Sara isn't going to invite me to her Valentine's Day party, I'm going to talk to her again.

I was thinking about Karl too.

I think he needs a friend.

I'm going to talk to him too.

Love,
Jessica

Alice

Thursday, February 14

Dear Miss Loria,

I've been sending letters to Private Helen Denning almost every day. She said the mail is slow there, and they wait and wait to get it.

You can read her letter yourself.

Mrs. Clark made copies.

She drew a heart on red paper, and tacked the letter to the bulletin board.

We tacked up a picture Helen sent, and one of Michael's father.

We're all going to keep writing. We'll send poems, and Jessica is even going to send her word list.

Love,
Alice

◆ Private Helen Denning ◆

Dear Alice,

   I hadn't gotten any mail for a week...and that's the most important thing for us here. We want to know what's going on at home.

   When two of your letters came, I put my feet up. I shared them with some of the others. We are looking forward to your package too.

   Listen, Alice, the thing that really keeps me going is thinking about all of you doing everyday things in school...studying, having snowball fights, going to birthday parties, having fun.

   I live in Massachusetts. That's not so far away. When I come home I'll take the train down to visit your class.

Love,
Helen Denning

P.S. Here's a picture of me on a jeep. See all the sand? I wish it were the beach.

Friday, February 15

Dear Miss Loria,

You know that Valentine party I told you about? It's not going to be a Valentine party anymore.

This is what happened.

This morning Mrs. Clark pinned BIRTHDAY STAR—ROOM 15 on Michael. His birthday is Sunday.

Michael didn't look happy though. He looked sad.

I guess he feels bad that his father won't be home.

Then I thought of something.

Instead of a Valentine party we could have a birthday party for Michael, the whole class at my house.

I went home right after school and my mother said yes. So that's what we're going to do.

Love,
Sara

♦ A Note from Jessica ♦

Friday, February 15

Dear Miss Loria,

Right after school Sara called. She's going to have a birthday party for Michael. The whole class is invited.

Sara and I are going shopping tomorrow morning to get him a present.

I don't know what. Michael likes such junky stuff.

Sara and I are best friends again. Isn't that the greatest fortune?

Love,
Jessica

Karl

Monday, February 18

Dear Miss Loria,

You missed a great party. It was for Michael.

Everyone jumped out and yelled SURPRISE! when he came.

Michael was happy.

He said he's going to have another party as soon as his father gets home.

You will be glad I'm not walking to school anymore.

I am taking the bus.

Jessica said the school bus is not going to get bombed. No way.

I'm really glad. I knew I had to leave Bigfoot home ever since Mrs. Baker talked to us.

It's my job to take care of him.

Jessica and I sat in back of the bus. We waved at Bigfoot.

He wagged his tail, then he picked up his ball and went around the side of the house.

He'll go in through the basement window and lie on the couch.

He'll be safe till I get home.

I can't wait to get to school today.

We're going to do something really important.

From,
Karl

◆ Sara ◆

Monday, February 18

Dear Miss Loria,

I'm glad we gave Michael that party.

He loved it.

He feels bad that his father isn't here, but he knows we are his friends.

We figured out something to do for the war.

Alice said to let her tell, so I will.

Love,
Sara

Alice

Monday, February 18

Dear Miss Loria,

We had the best time at Michael's party. His mother came, and his grandmother, and even Mrs. Clark.

Michael showed me the card his father sent him. It said that Michael and his father were going to a baseball game when he comes home. It said that when his father comes home, he'll never miss another birthday until Michael has a long white beard.

Michael and I laughed about that.

I told Michael I was sorry for that fight we had.

Michael said it was all right. He looked sad for a minute, then he started eating.

That Michael eats a lot. I think he ate half the cake himself. After a while, he opened his presents. He got a whole pile.

Jessica thinks he likes hers the best. It's a little red racing car. (I think he has about a thousand, but I didn't tell Jessica that.)

66

Afterward everyone started to talk about the war.

Someone said remember Helen's letter? And someone else said she'd love to hear about the birthday party.

Karl got the greatest idea.

He said he's going to draw some pictures for Helen. Pictures of everyday things, just like she said in her letter.

Mrs. Clark said Karl was certainly using his head.

Jessica said she was going to use her head too.

She was going to draw the racing car she got Michael.

Anyway, we're going to do a mural today.

We're going to draw in all the things we do.

Michael and Sara are going to draw the party with the cake and Michael's grandmother wearing a birthday hat.

Karl is going to draw Bigfoot playing with his ball.

I'm going to do a snowman I built in my yard. He's wearing a yellow ribbon, and he's melting only a little.

We're going to send the mural to Helen. We're going to send one next week, too, and the week after.

We're going to keep sending them until the war is over. I hope it's soon, don't you?

Love,
Alice

ABOUT THE AUTHOR

PATRICIA REILLY GIFF is the author of many books for children, including the Kids of the Polk Street School; the Casey, Tracy, and Company; and the Polka Dot Private Eye books. A former teacher and reading consultant, she holds degrees from Marymount College and St. John's University and a Professional Diploma in Reading and a Doctorate of Humane Letters from Hofstra University. She wrote this book because she was a child during World War II and remembers what it was like to be confused and afraid of a war happening far away. She lives in Weston, Connecticut.

ABOUT THE ILLUSTRATOR

Betsy Lewin has illustrated many books for children, including *What If the Shark Wears Tennis Shoes*. She lives in Brooklyn, New York.